P9-DDB-071

OLD MOTHER HUBBARD
AND HER WONDERFUL DOG

ILLUSTRATED BY
JAMES MARSHALL

FARRAR, STRAUS AND GIROUX

NEW YORK

E
MAR

Old Mother Hubbard
Went to the cupboard,
To fetch her poor dog a bone;

But when she came there
The cupboard was bare
And so the poor dog had none.

She went to the baker
To buy him some bread;

But when she came back
The poor dog was dead.

She went to the undertaker
To buy him a coffin;

But when she came back
  The poor dog was laughing.

She took a clean dish
To get him some tripe;

But when she came back
He was smoking a pipe.

She went to the fishmonger
To buy him some fish;

But when she came back
He was licking his dish.

She went to the tavern
For white wine and red;

But when she came back
The dog stood on his head.

She went to the fruit stand
To buy him some fruit;

But when she came back
He was playing the flute.

She went to the tailor
To buy him a coat;

She went to the hatter
To buy him a hat;

But when she got back
   He was feeding the cat.

She went to the barber
To buy him a wig;

She went to the cobbler
To buy him some shoes;

But when she came back
   He was reading the news.

She went to the seamstress
To buy him some linen;

But when she came back
The dog was a-spinning.

She went to the hosier
To buy him some hose;

But when she came back

He was dressed in his clothes.
The dame made a curtsey,
The dog made a bow;

The dame said, Your servant,
The dog said:

The dame said, Your servant,
The dog said:

For Michael di Capua

Copyright © 1991 by James Marshall

All rights reserved

Library of Congress catalog card number: 90-56145

Published simultaneously in Canada by HarperCollins*CanadaLtd*

Color separations by Imago Publishing Ltd.

Printed and bound in the United States of America by

Horowitz/Rae Book Manufacturers

Typography by Cynthia Krupat

First edition, 1991